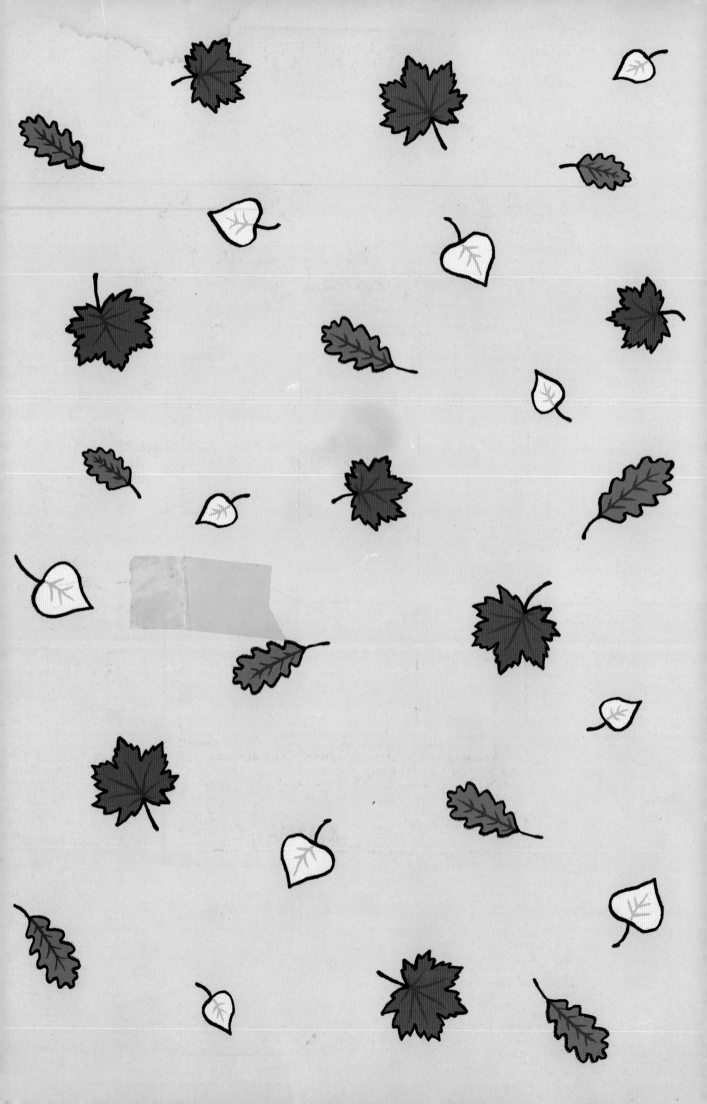

Shark in the Park on a Windy Day!

With thanks to all the children who helped me
with ideas for this book, especially Husnain Javid
and the pupils at St John the Baptist CE VC
Primary School, Stockton-on-Tees

MIX
Paper from
responsible sources
FSC
www.fsc.org   FSC® C018179

Penguin Random House is committed to a sustainable future for
our business, our readers and our planet. This book is made from
Forest Stewardship Council® certified paper.

SHARK IN THE PARK ON A WINDY DAY
A PICTURE CORGI BOOK 978 0 552 57310 8

Published in Great Britain by Picture Corgi,
an imprint of Random House Children's Publishers UK
A Penguin Random House Company

Penguin
Random House
UK

This edition published 2015

1 3 5 7 9 10 8 6 4 2

Copyright © Nick Sharratt, 2015

The right of Nick Sharratt to be identified as the author and illustrator of this work
has been asserted in accordance with the Copyright, Designs and Patents Act 1988.

Picture Corgi Books are published by Random House Children's Publishers UK,
61–63 Uxbridge Road, London W5 5SA

www.randomhousechildrens.co.uk
www.randomhouse.co.uk

Addresses for companies within The Random House Group Limited can be found at:
www.randomhouse.co.uk/offices.htm

THE RANDOM HOUSE GROUP Limited Reg. No. 954009

A CIP catalogue record for this book is available from the British Library.

Printed in China

Shark in the Park on a Windy Day!

Nick
Sharratt

PICTURE CORGI

It's a **wild**, **windy** day
and a certain small boy
is out with his dad
and his favourite toy.

. . . because this is what he sees!

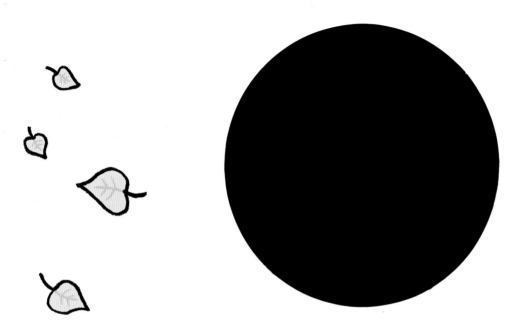

Tim knows that shape
and he knows what to do.
He shouts,

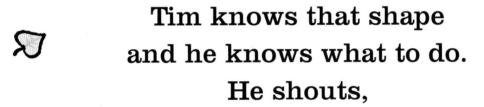

**"SHARK IN
THE PARK!"**

Can you shout that out too?

It isn't a shark
that Timothy sees . . .

. . . it's a big, black umbrella
caught up in the breeze!

. . . because this is what he sees!

Oh dear me!
Tim's got no choice,
he shouts,

"SHARK IN THE PARK!"

at the top of his voice.

What a relief! It isn't a shark.

. . . because this is what he sees!

Timothy does
what he knows he must –
he shouts,

"SHARK IN
THE PARK!"

till he's fit to bust!

"Really," says Tim's dad,
"You ought to thank Tim.
He spotted your pram
so it's all down to him!"